Menchi and the Colourful Puppy

The Meet Menchi Series

D. J. HUGHES

Menchi the Colourful Puppy
THE MEET MENCHI SERIES

iUniverse books may be ordered through booksellers or by contacting:

iUniverse
1663 Liberty Drive
Bloomington, IN 47403
www.iuniverse.com
1-800-Authors (1-800-288-4677)

Because of the dynamic nature of the internet, any web addresses or links contained in this book may have changed since publication and may no longer be valid. The views expressed in this work are solely those of the author and do not necessarily reflect the views of the publisher, and the publisher hereby disclaims any responsibility for them.

Any people depicted in stock imagery provided by Getty Images are models,
and such images are being used for illustrative purposes only.
Certain stock imagery © Getty Images.

ISBN: 978-1-6632-0345-8 (sc)
ISBN: 978-1-6632-0346-5 (e)

Library of Congress Control Number: 2020911519

Printed in the United States of America.

iUniverse rev. date: 07/11/2020

Menchi the Colourful Puppy

Menchi is a colourful pup; she likes to play all day.

Menchi is a light brown pup; she
loves to chase her tail and play.

Menchi has a pink collar and wears it like a bow.

Menchi has a red tongue and moves it to and fro.

Menchi has yellow on her nose from
smelling the bright flowers.

Menchi has green grass on her back
from rolling around for hours.

Menchi has grey paws; she was born that way.

Menchi has a black nose; she
thinks it's here to stay.

Menchi has brown eyes under her pink sunglasses.

Menchi has an orange tag that
jangles when she passes.

Menchi has a purple coat; she wears it in a storm.

Menchi has blue boots; they
keep her toes very warm.

Menchi has a purple hat; it covers both her ears.

Menchi wears spotted scarfs;
she will wear them for years.

Menchi is a funny pup with many stories to tell.

Menchi is a colourful pup;
she wears her colours well.

Menchi was once a homeless dog. She loves adventure,
travel, her people and learning new things.

Through her adventures you will *see* what a caring
family can do for her or any homeless animal.

Menchi wants to talk to you about how she found a home.

Because of her new family, she always has a bone.

So go and look at shelters for all the dogs and cats.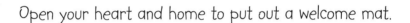

Open your heart and home to put out a welcome mat.

Please adopt a pet if you can.

Homeless pets are alone and scared, and they need a family home.

Thank you from your friend Menchi,

the dog that grows with you.

A portion of the profits from this *book* goes
toward supporting local animal shelters.